Nix Kerberos

Charon

Hydra

Saturn

Uranus

Neptune

Pluto

For Len, who loves planets
—G. P.

For Joe, who likes to think
big thoughts
—R. G.

MARGARET K. McELDERRY BOOKS
An imprint of Simon & Schuster Children's Publishing Division
• 1230 Avenue of the Americas, New York, New York 10020 •
Text copyright © 2019 by Gabrielle Prendergast • Illustrations
copyright © 2019 by Rebecca Gerlings • All rights reserved,
including the right of reproduction in whole or in part in any form.
• MARGARET K. McELDERRY BOOKS is a trademark of Simon &
Schuster, Inc. • For information about special discounts for
bulk purchases, please contact Simon & Schuster Special Sales
at 1-866-506-1949 or business@simonandschuster.com. • The
Simon & Schuster Speakers Bureau can bring authors to your
live event. For more information or to book an event, contact
the Simon & Schuster Speakers Bureau at 1-866-248-3049 or
visit our website at www.simonspeakers.com. • Book design
by Sonia Chaghatzbanian • The text for this book was set in
Century Gothic. • The illustrations for this book were rendered
digitally. • Manufactured in China • 0619 SCP • First Edition •
10 9 8 7 6 5 4 3 2 1 • Library of Congress Cataloging-
in-Publication Data • Names: Prendergast, Gabrielle, author.
| Gerlings, Rebecca, illustrator. • Title: If Pluto was a pea /
Gabrielle Prendergast ; illustrated by Rebecca Gerlings. •
Description: First edition. | New York : Margaret K. McElderry
Books, [2019] | Audience: Ages 4-8. | Summary: "Pluto is the
smallest planet in our solar system, but how small is small?
Join two curious kids as they explore their backyard, and
contemplate their place within our vast universe."— Provided
by publisher. • Identifiers: LCCN 2018026421 (print) | LCCN
2018034328 (eBook) | ISBN 9781534404366 (eBook) | ISBN
9781534404359 (hardcover) • Subjects: LCSH: Pluto (Dwarf
planet)—Juvenile literature. | Planets—Juvenile literature. |
Size perception—Juvenile literature. | Solar system—Juvenile
literature. • Classification: LCC QB701 (eBook) | LCC QB701
.P74 2019 (print) | DDC 523.49/22—dc23 • LC record available
at https://lccn.loc.gov/2018026421

If Pluto Was a Pea

by Gabrielle Prendergast

illustrated by Rebecca Gerlings

McElderry Books • New York London Toronto Sydney New Delhi

Pluto is much smaller than the other planets. That's why it's called a "Dwarf Planet."

But how much smaller is it?

If **Pluto** was a pea
(0.64 centimeters or
0.25 inches),

the sun would be a tent
(4 meters or 13 feet).

If **Pluto** was a pea,

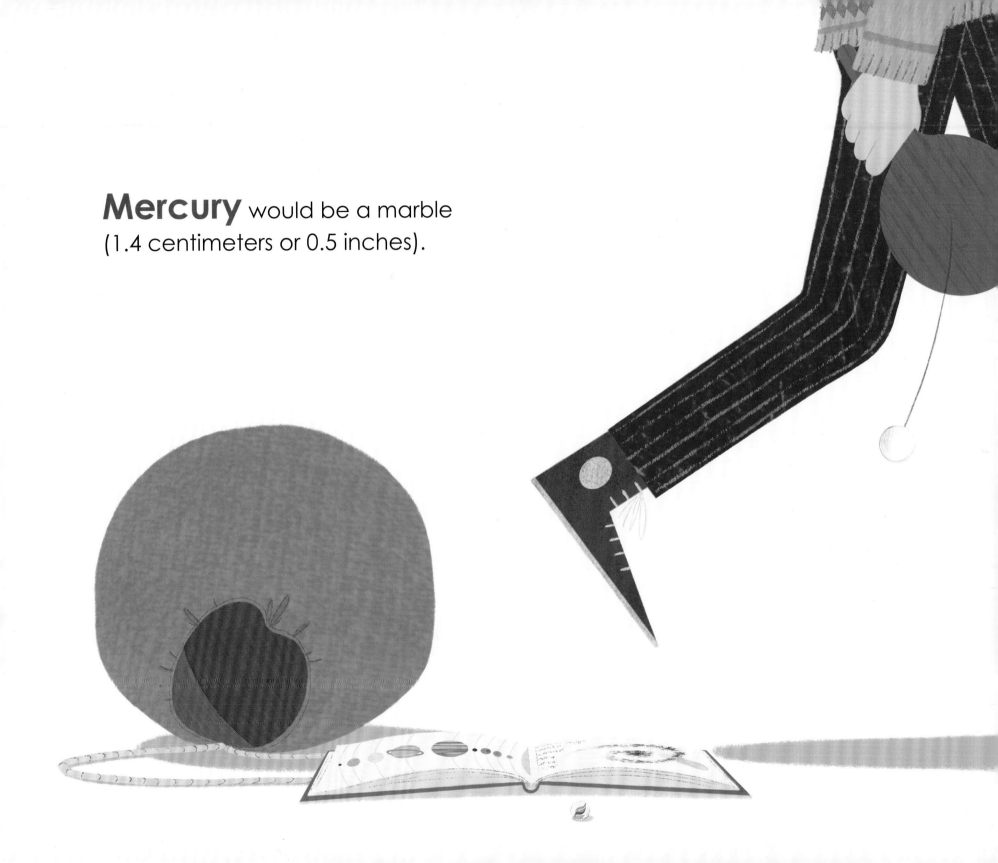

Mercury would be a marble (1.4 centimeters or 0.5 inches).

If **Pluto** was a pea,

Venus would be a Ping-Pong ball
(3.4 centimeters or 1.3 inches).

If **Pluto** was a pea,

the **Earth** would be a golf ball
(3.52 centimeters or 1.4 inches).

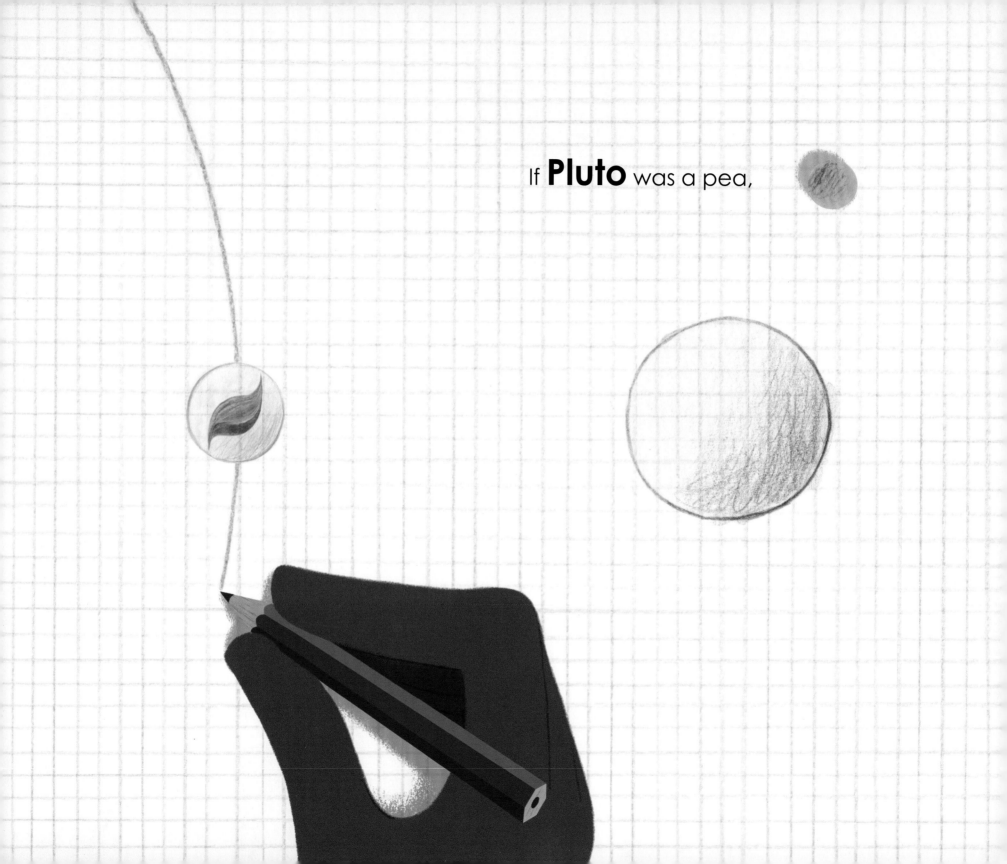

If **Pluto** was a pea,

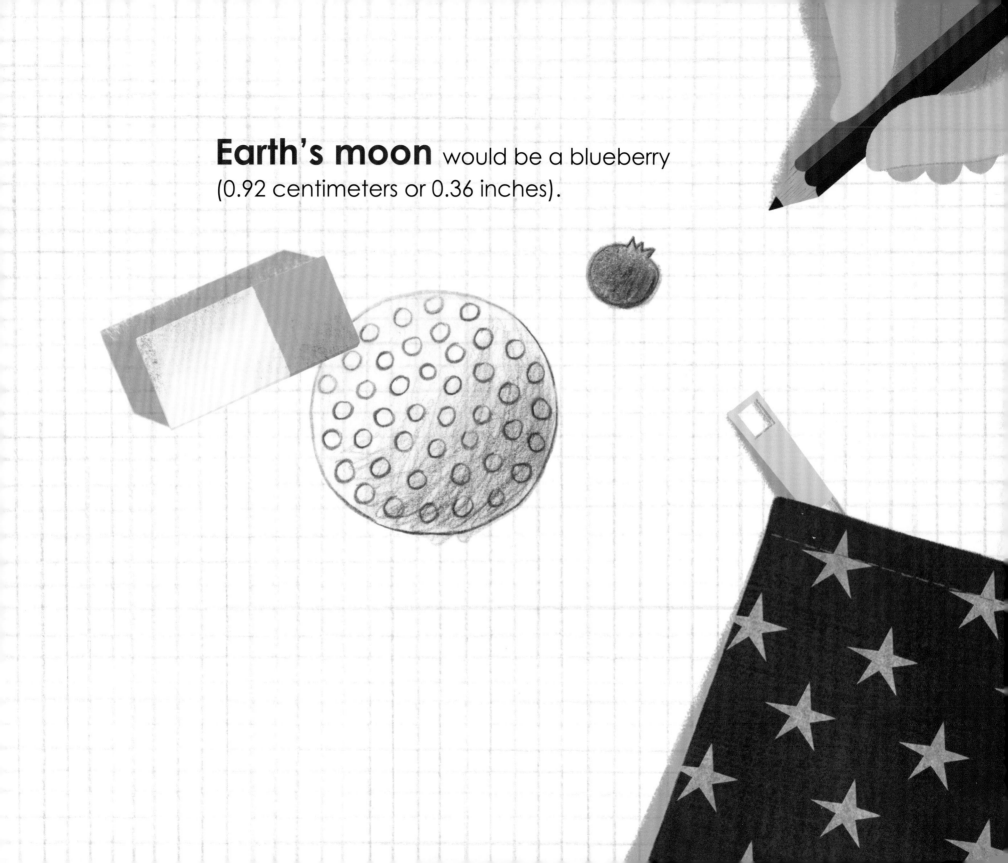

Earth's moon would be a blueberry (0.92 centimeters or 0.36 inches).

If **Pluto** was a pea,

Mars would be an acorn
(1.9 centimeters or 0.75 inches).

If **Pluto** was a pea,

Jupiter would be a beach ball (40 centimeters or 15.75 inches).

If **Pluto** was a pea,

Saturn would be a pumpkin
(33 centimeters or 13 inches).

If **Pluto** was a pea,

Uranus would be a melon
(14.27 centimeters or 5.6 inches).

If **Pluto** was a pea,

Neptune would be a grapefruit
(13.76 centimeters or 5.4 inches).

Is **Pluto** smaller than everything in the **Solar System**?

No!

If **Pluto** was a pea,

her own moon, **Charon**, would be an apple seed (0.3 centimeters or 0.12 inches).

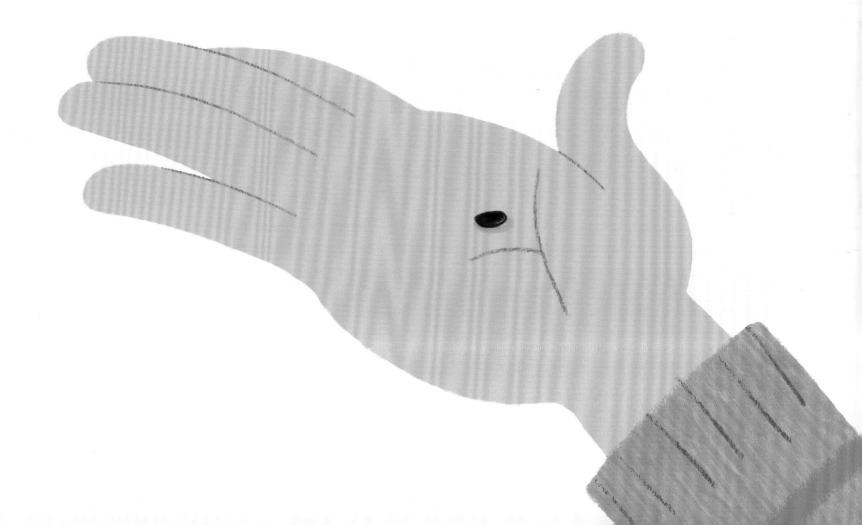

If **Pluto** was a pea,

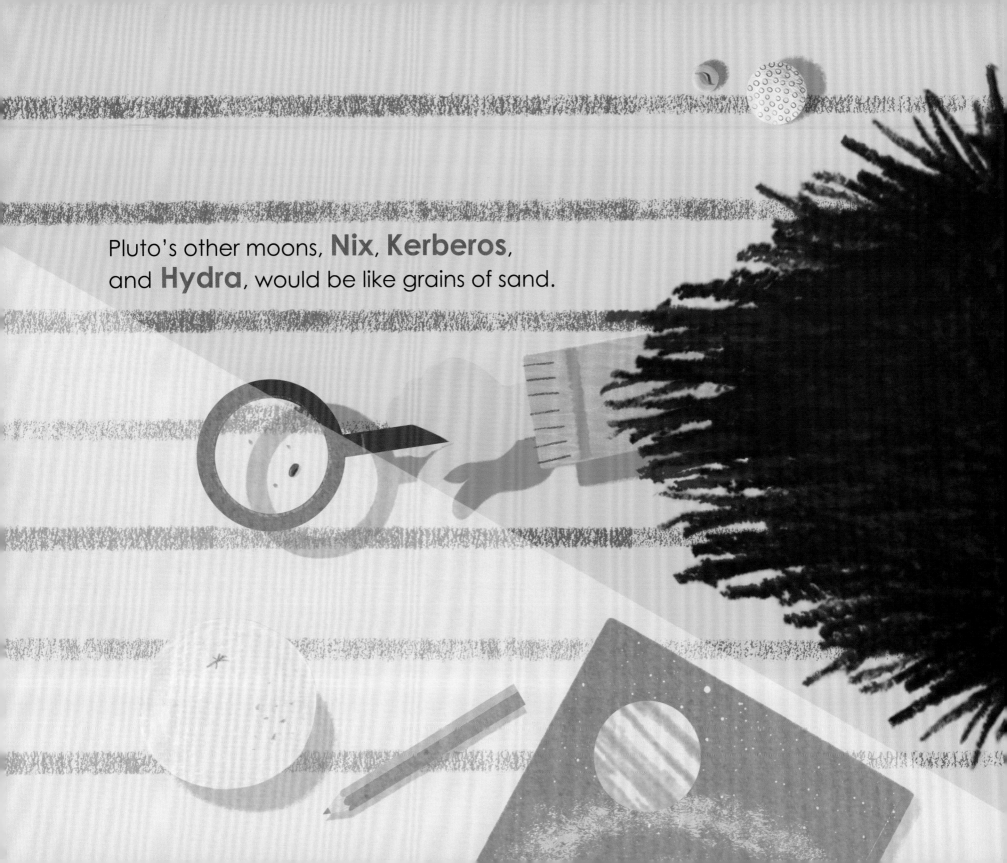

Pluto's other moons, **Nix**, **Kerberos**, and **Hydra**, would be like grains of sand.

If **Pluto** was a pea,

Pluto's smallest moon, **Styx**,
would be too small to see.

And **YOU** would be much,
much smaller than that.

But still not too small to think **big** thoughts
and do **great** things.

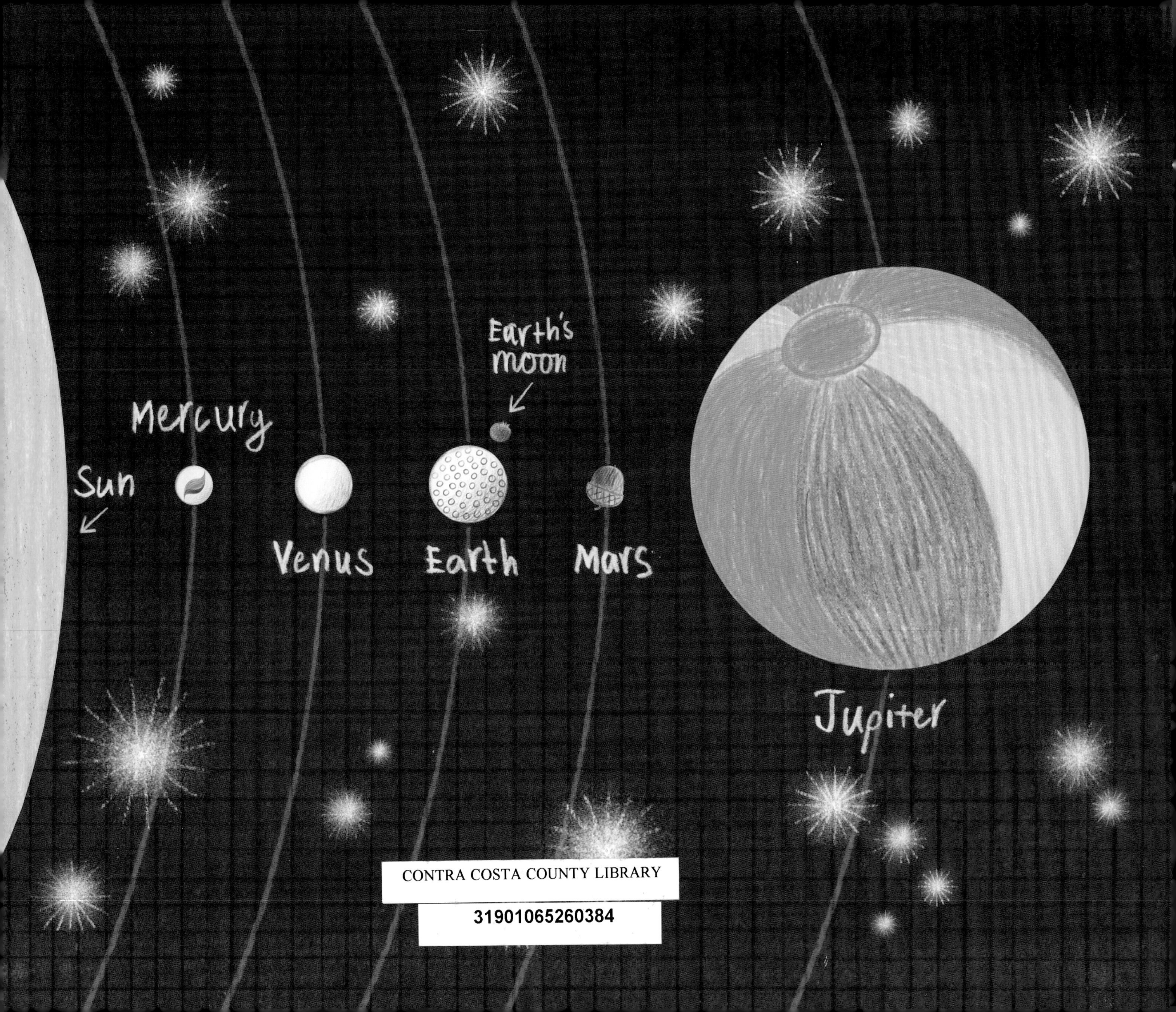

Sun

Mercury

Venus

Earth

Earth's moon

Mars

Jupiter